+47668

Weekly Reader Presents

If I Were King of the Universe

By Danny Abelson · Pictures by Lawrence DiFiori

Muppet Press
Henry Holt and Company
NEW YORK

Published by Henry Holt and Company,
521 Fifth Avenue, New York, New York 10175

Library of Congress Cataloging in Publication Data
Abelson, Danny, 1950-
If I were king of the universe.
Summary: An overworked Prince Gorg dreams of being king.
[1. Puppets—Fiction. 2. Stories in rhyme]
I. Di Fiori, Lawrence, ill. II. Title.
PZ8.3.A128If 1984 [E] 83-22708
ISBN 0-03-071087-1

Printed in the United States of America

ISBN 0-03-071087-1

This book is a presentation of
Weekly Reader Books

If I Were King of the Universe

Hello, there! Allow me to introduce myself. My name is Junior Gorg. My Pa is King of the Universe, and my Ma is Queen. So that makes me Prince of the Universe!

Ma and Pa spend most of their time ruling over all the Gorgs. Don't they make a handsome couple?

Unfortunately, as far as we know, I'm the only other Gorg in the universe. That means Ma and Pa rule over me—and **that** means I have to do most of the chores around here.

I wash the royal windows, I polish Pa's armor, and I sweep out the hall. When Ma wants the royal jewels, I fetch them for her. I guard the castle in case of attack, I'm the court jester, and I even take care of the royal accounts.

But my favorite chore of all is gardening. I grow the biggest, juiciest, most beautiful radishes in the entire universe! If the universe held a radish-growing competition, I know my radishes would win first prize, second prize, **and** third prize.

That's why I get so mad at those pesky Fraggles. They're always coming into my garden and running off with my radishes. Hey, Fraggles! Come back here!

If I really wanted to protect my beautiful radishes from those nasty Fraggles, I would have to stand guard day and night!

But I can't stay in the garden. Ma and Pa are always calling me for something. When Pa decides he's hungry and yells for his supper, do you know who has to set the table? You guessed it! Me!

I love my Ma and my Pa. But sometimes I don't feel like doing all my chores. I don't feel like polishing or sweeping or scrubbing or fetching or guarding. Sometimes I wish that . . . that . . . I were King of the Universe!

If I were king, all the other Gorgs would bow down to me and obey my every command! (That is, they would if there were any other Gorgs besides Ma, Pa, and me.)

Instead of stealing my radishes, the Fraggles would all work for me. I'd make them do the gardening. That way, I could play all day long!

Ma would serve me breakfast in bed, and I could eat all the things she says are bad for me—even chocolate pudding topped with marshmallows and strawberries. Yum!

I would lie around all day long if I felt like it, just talking to my toes in the sun. Hello, toes! How are you feeling today?

I would stay up late every night, and make Ma and Pa go to bed before nine. They would obey me, because I would be Junior Gorg, King of the Universe!

And then I'd . . . and then I'd . . . I'd . . . You know, I simply can't think of a thing to do next. Can you?

I spent my whole day watching Ma and Pa do the chores and the Fraggles do the gardening. Everybody was doing something except for me. Now everybody is asleep, and the truth is . . . I'm bored!

I guess I like doing my chores. Chasing Fraggles is really a lot of fun. What's more, Ma and Pa really depend on me. What would Pa do without me to shine his armor? How could Ma get along if I didn't help her brush out her hair every night?

So I guess I'll go back to being plain Junior Gorg.
I'll take care of the radishes, eat oatmeal for breakfast,
and be in bed at nine. Ma and Pa will be proud of me!

After all, being Prince of the Universe isn't all that bad!